For Ben, Katie, and Tom Goble
and for Samuel, Anna, and Rachael Hor

Paul Goble Gallery

THREE NATIVE AMERICAN STORIES

Simon & Schuster
Books for Young Readers

ALSO BY PAUL GOBLE

Adopted by the Eagles
Beyond the Ridge
Brave Eagle's Account of the Fetterman Fight
Buffalo Woman
Crow Chief
Death of the Iron Horse
Dream Wolf
The Friendly Wolf
The Gift of the Sacred Dog
The Girl Who Loved Wild Horses
The Great Race of the Birds and Animals
Hau Kola, Hello Friend (autobiography for children)
Her Seven Brothers
I Sing for the Animals
Iktomi and the Berries
Iktomi and the Boulder
Iktomi and the Buffalo Skull
Iktomi and the Buzzard
Iktomi and the Coyote
Iktomi and the Ducks
The Legend of the White Buffalo Woman
Lone Bull's Horse Raid
The Lost Children
Love Flute
Red Hawk's Account of Custer's Last Battle
Remaking the Earth
The Return of the Buffaloes
Star Boy

SIMON & SCHUSTER
BOOKS FOR YOUNG READERS
An imprint of Simon & Schuster Children's Publishing Division
1230 Avenue of the Americas
New York, New York 10020
Paul Goble Gallery copyright © 1999 by Paul Goble
All rights reserved including the right of
reproduction in whole or in part in any form.
Her Seven Brothers copyright © 1988 by Paul Goble
The Gift of the Sacred Dog copyright © 1980 by Paul Goble
The Girl Who Loved Wild Horses copyright © 1978 by Paul Goble
SIMON & SCHUSTER BOOKS FOR YOUNG READERS
is a trademark of Simon & Schuster.
The text of this book is set in Bembo.
Printed in Hong Kong
10 9 8 7 6 5 4 3 2 1
ISBN 0-689-82219-7
Library of Congress Card Catalog Number: 98-88492

first
edition

INTRODUCTION

I wrote and illustrated *The Gift of the Sacred Dog* and *The Girl Who Loved Wild Horses* after I had read and listened to a great number of stories belonging to the many peoples who lived on the Great Plains. Neither book follows any one story exactly. I have had Indian people tell me that both of them "capture the spirit" of their stories, or that they recognize them as stories which they've been told. I am glad they feel this, because every detail came from the various stories I had read or heard. But in the books that I wrote after these two, I kept to a specific myth. *Her Seven Brothers* comes from the Cheyennes.

I use the word "myth" in its true sense of "sacred story," which traditional Native American stories are. The word "myth" has come to mean a fairy tale created to entertain children, but traditional myths of peoples all over the world have always conveyed truths, using the symbols and idioms of their particular times and places. Like Bible stories, their meanings need to be sensed and meditated upon. It took me a while to realize that these Native American stories are greater than anything I could imagine, and that it was wrong to invent. I have felt that my work was to try to pass them on from one culture to another, in pictures and words, and to still keep something of the spirit of the originals. What a *long* way it is, even for Indian peoples today, from the tipi to the apartment; from the thinking of nomadic hunters to TV talk shows, stone age to plastic; from oral to written, the mind's eye to a picture book.

People have often asked me which of these stories is my favorite. I love them all, but the "favorite" is always the one I am working on. It may be one I have known for years. Probably I have read it in several versions, the best of which were recorded from Indian people about a hundred years ago. Possibly I have heard it told, although, sadly, some of these stories have been forgotten. And then thinking about it one day, I will suddenly feel I glimpse some important meaning. From that point on, I feel able to retell it, and it is my "favorite"! It has to be, in order to find the self-motivation to keep with the writing and illustrating over a period of many months.

It has been a joy and privilege, and continuing education, to work and meditate on these Indian stories. In some Oriental traditions a person's life is likened to a journey, a climb along the Way which leads up toward the summit of a distant snow-capped Mountain, which is Perfection, God, the ultimate destination. I think all of us can look at our working or creative lives in this way. If we stay on the Way, keeping the Mountain in sight, and do not falter in concentration, perhaps we will climb out of the valley; we may leave the trees behind and reach the snow-line, and perhaps even be rewarded with a closer view of the summit. Isn't looking at old work like looking back at our trail along the Way we have climbed? We are glad to have got thus far, and would not want to have to climb it all again! They were steps which brought us to where we are now. When I think of the happy years of work on the books, my beloved wife, Janet, with me, it really *is* like looking back at foot-tracks along the Way.

Paul Goble
Rapid City, South Dakota

Her Seven Brothers

For Robert

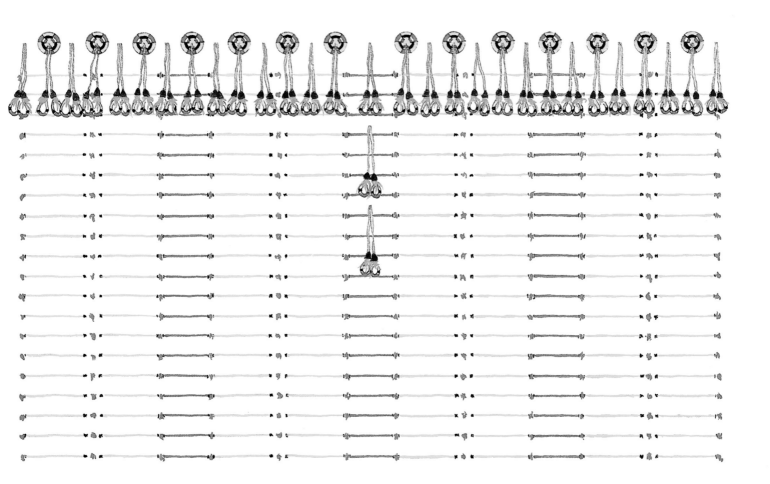

A NOTE FROM THE AUTHOR

The designs of the shirts and dresses and various other articles in this book are based on Cheyenne designs. These articles can be seen in many museums in both the United States and Europe. The designs of the painted tipis are taken from models that were made by Cheyennes about 1900 for the Field Museum of Natural History in Chicago.

The birds and animals, the flowers and butterflies share the earth with us, and so they are included in the pictures. Sometimes two of each are drawn; they, like us, enjoy each other's company. In other places many are drawn, reminding us of the Creator's generosity. They all live on the Great Plains, where this story takes place.

The illustrations are drawn with pen and India ink. When a drawing is finished, it looks much like a page from a child's painting book. The drawings are then filled in with watercolor, which is often applied rather thickly. Thin white lines are left, to try and achieve the brightness of Indian bead and quillwork, and to capture something of the bright colors that one sees in the clear air of the Great Plains.

References for this Cheyenne story: Richard Erdoes and Alfonso Ortiz, *American Indian Myths and Legends,* Pantheon Books, New York, 1984; George Bird Grinnell, *By Cheyenne Campfires,* Yale University Press, New Haven, 1926; John Stands in Timber and Margot Liberty, *Cheyenne Memories,* Yale University Press, New Haven, 1967; A. L. Kroeber, "Cheyenne Tales," *The Journal of American Folk-lore,* Vol. XIII, No. 1, 1900; Carrie A. Lyford, *Quill and Beadwork of the Western Sioux,* Washington, DC, 1940; Alice Marriott, *The Trade Guild of the Southern Cheyenne Women,* Oklahoma Anthropological Society, 1937.

STORIES were told after dark when the mind's eye sees most clearly. Winter evenings were best, when the children were lying under their buffalo robes and the fire was glowing at the center of the tipi. After the sounds in the camp had grown quiet and the deer had come out to graze, the storyteller would smooth the earth in front of him; rubbing his hands together, he would pass them over his head and body. He was remembering that the Creator had made people out of the earth, and would be witness to the truth of the story he was going to tell.

DO you know what the birds and animals say?
In the old days there were more people who understood them. The Creator did not intend them to speak in our way; theirs is the language of the spirits. Yes, birds and animals, butterflies and beetles, stones and trees still speak to us; but we have to learn how to listen.

In those distant times there was a girl who lived with her parents. She did not have any brothers or sisters, but she was never alone because she could speak with the birds and animals. She understood the spirits of all things.

When the girl was quite young her mother taught her how to embroider with dyed porcupine quills onto deer and buffalo skin robes and clothes. She worked hard. In time she became very good at it. Her parents were proud when she gave away something she had made. People marveled at her skill and beautiful designs. They believed that Porcupine, who climbs trees closest to Sun himself, had spoken to the girl and given her mysterious help to do such wonderful work. While the girl worked, she kept good thoughts in her mind; she knew that she could not make anything beautiful without help from the spirits.

One day she started to sew clothes for a man: a shirt and a pair
of moccasins. She decorated them with porcupine quills in brightly
colored patterns. Every design had a meaning for her.

When the shirt and moccasins were finished, she did not give
them to anyone; she put them away and started on another set.
Her parents wondered why she did this when she had neither
brothers nor young men who were courting her. When a second
set was finished and she was starting another, her mother asked
her for whom she was making the clothes.

Her daughter replied: "There are seven brothers who live by
themselves far in the north country where the cold wind comes
from. I have seen them in my mind when I close my eyes. I am
making the clothes for them. They have no sister. I will look for the
trail that leads to their tipi. I will ask them to be my brothers."

At first her mother thought it was just a young girl's imagining, but every day her daughter brought out her work. The months passed, and she made six shirts and pairs of moccasins. And then she started with special care on a seventh set, smaller than the others, to fit a very small boy. Her mother was puzzled, and yet she sensed that her daughter had seen something wonderful. Even the wise men did not know, but they believed that the unseen powers had spoken to the girl.

Her mother said: "I will go with you. When the snow melts we will pack your gifts onto the dogs. I will help you guide them until you find the trail."

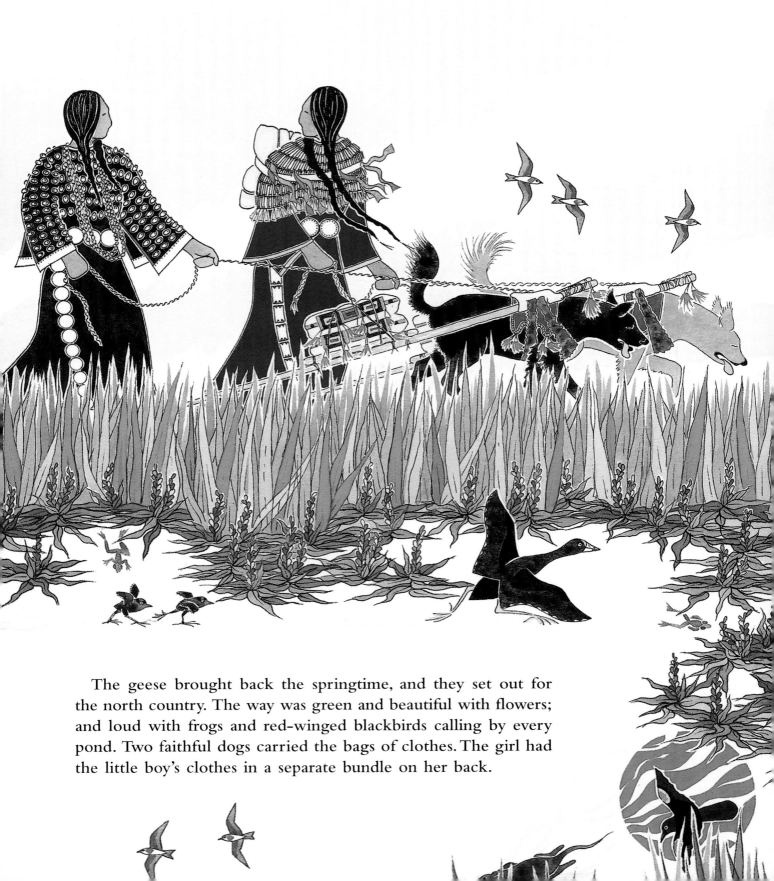

The geese brought back the springtime, and they set out for the north country. The way was green and beautiful with flowers; and loud with frogs and red-winged blackbirds calling by every pond. Two faithful dogs carried the bags of clothes. The girl had the little boy's clothes in a separate bundle on her back.

When the girl found the trail, she said to her mother: "This is where I will go on alone. Mother, do not be sad! You will be proud! Soon you will see me again with my brothers; everyone will know and love us!"

But her mother did cry. She called to the sun: "O Sun, look after my child!" She watched her daughter, leading a dog at either hand, walk away and fade slowly into the immensity of the blue distance.

The girl walked on for many days into the land of pine trees until she came at last to a tipi pitched close to a lake. It was painted yellow and had stars all over it. The door was partly open; she thought she could see bright eyes peering at her from inside.

She unpacked the bags from the dogs. After they had taken a drink at the lake, she thanked them. "Now go straight back home," she told them. "Keep to the trail, and do not chase rabbits."

A little boy ran out of the tipi and called to her: "I am glad you have come! I have been waiting for you! You have come looking for brothers. I have six older brothers. They are away hunting buffalo, but they will be back this evening. They will be surprised to see you; they do not have my power of knowing and seeing. I am glad to call you 'Sister.'"

The girl opened the bundle of clothes she had made for him. "Younger Brother," she said, "this is my gift to you."

The boy had never seen anything so beautiful; his clothes had always been plain, and often old. He put on his new shirt and moccasins and scampered down to the lake to take a look at himself in the water. The girl untied the other bags, and placed a shirt and pair of moccasins on each of the six beds around the tipi.

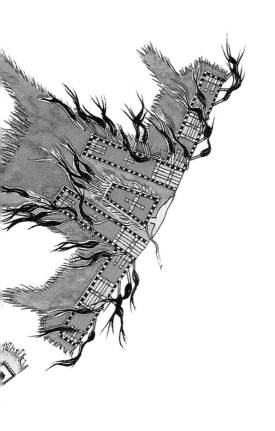

When the little boy heard his brothers returning, he ran out of the tipi to meet them. "Wherever did you get those fine clothes?" they asked.

The boy replied: "A girl made them for me. She came looking for brothers, and now I call her 'Sister.' She has made wonderful shirts for all of you. Come and see!"

The brothers were very proud of their sister and looked after her well. While they were out hunting, she stayed in the tipi with the little boy. He would take his bow and arrows to protect her if she went out for water or to gather firewood. She liked to have good meals ready for the hunters when they returned home.

They all lived happily together until a day when a little buffalo calf came to the tipi. He scratched at the door with his hoof. The boy went outside and asked: "What do you want, Buffalo Calf?"

"I have been sent by the Chief of the Buffalo Nation," the calf said. "He wants your sister. Tell her to follow me."

"He cannot have her," the boy answered. "My sister is happy here. We are proud of her."

The calf ran away, but in a little while a yearling bull galloped up to the tipi and bellowed: "I have been sent by the Chief of the Buffalo Nation. He insists on having your sister. Tell her to come."

"No! He will never have her," the boy answered. "Go away!"

It was not long before an old bull with sharp curved horns charged up and thundered: "The Chief of the Buffalo Nation demands your sister *now*! She must come *at once*, or he will come with the whole Buffalo Nation and get her, and you will all be killed." He shook his mane and whipped his back with his tail in rage.

"No!" the boy shouted. "He will never have her. Look! There are my big brothers coming back. *Hurry,* or they will surely kill you!"

When the brothers heard what had happened they were afraid.
Even then they sensed an uncertain rumble, like shaking deep
down inside the earth. Beyond the horizon dark dust clouds were
rolling out across the sky toward them. The Buffalo People were
stampeding in the awful darkness beneath.

"Run!" shouted one of the brothers.

"Wait!" the little boy called out, and he ran into the tipi for his bow and arrows. He shot an arrow straight up into the air and a pine tree appeared, growing upward with the arrow's flight.

The girl quickly lifted her little brother onto the lowest branch and climbed up after him. All the brothers clambered after, just as the Chief of the Buffalo Nation struck the tree a terrible blow, splintering it with his horns. He hooked at the trunk again and again and it was split into slivers. Dark masses of angry buffalo crowded around the tree, pawing the ground and bellowing. The tree quivered and started to topple.

"Hurry! You have power. Save us!" the brothers called to the little boy. He shot an arrow and the tree grew taller.

He shot another far into the sky and the tree grew straight upward, higher and higher, and they were carried far away up among the stars.

And there they all jumped down from the branches onto the boundless star-prairies of the world above.

THE girl and her seven brothers are still there. They are the Seven Stars in the northern sky, which we call the Big Dipper. But look carefully and you will see that there are really eight stars in the Big Dipper; close to one of them there is a tiny star; it is the little boy walking with his sister. She is never lonely now. They are forever turning around the Star Which Always Stands Still, the North Star. It is good to know that they once lived here on earth.

Listen to the stars! We are never alone at night.

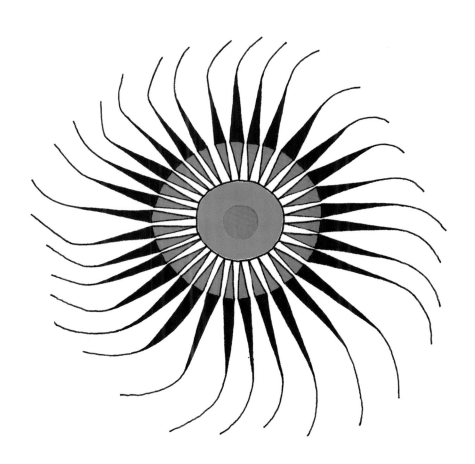

The Gift of the Sacred Dog

ABOUT THE TITLE

Horses were brought to North America by the Spanish. To the tribes of nomadic buffalo hunters who lived on the Great Plains, horses were truly miraculous. This wonderful animal could not only carry and drag far heavier burdens than their dogs, but could also carry a rider and run faster than anyone ever imagined. The tribes call him by various names: Big Dog, Elk Dog, Mysterious Dog, Holy or Sacred Dog. They tell factual accounts of the first horses they saw, but the story is told as well in ways which remind that Sacred Dogs were indeed given by the Great Spirit.

REFERENCES

The Gift of the Sacred Dog and *The Girl Who Loved Wild Horses* grew out of study, and listening to and reading traditional stories of Native American peoples who lived on the Great Plains. The books listed below are a sampling of some of the earliest sources, recorded during the early 1900s from Indian people who had lived during Buffalo Days. These are the closest we can get to the traditions of those early times. Many of these collections, and others by the same authors, are available in modern editions:
Natalie Curtis, *The Indians' Book,* Harper and Brothers, New York, 1907; Ella C. Deloria, *Dakota Texts,* vol 14, Publications of the American Ethnology Society, New York, 1932; George Amos Dorsey and Alfred L. Kroeber, *Traditions of the Arapaho,* Field Museum of Natural History, Anthropological Series, vol 5, Chicago, 1903; James Own Dorsey, *A Study of Siouan Cults,* Eleventh Annual Report, Bureau of American Ethnology, Washington, DC, 1894; Charles Eastman (Ohiyesa), *Wigwam Evenings,* Little, Brown, Boston, 1909; George Bird Grinnell, *By Cheyenne Campfires,* Yale University Press, New Haven, 1926; *Blackfoot Lodge Tales,* Charles Scribner's Sons, New York, 1892; *Pawnee Hero Stories and Folk-Tales,* Forest and Stream Publishing Co., New York, 1889; Alfred L. Kroeber, *Cheyenne Tales,* vol 13, Journal of American Folk-Lore, New York, 1900; Robert H. Lowie, *Myths and Traditions of the Crow Indians,* Anthropological Papers of the American Museum of Natural History, vol 25, pt 1, New York, 1918; Walter McClintock, *The Old North Trail: Life, Legends and Religion of the Blackfeet Indians,* Macmillan, London, 1910; Luther Standing Bear, *Stories of the Sioux,* Houghton Mifflin, Boston, 1934; Stith Thompson, *Tales of the North American Indians,* Indiana University Press, Bloomington, 1929; Clark Wissler and D. C. Duvall, *Mythology of the Blackfoot Indians,* Anthropological Papers of the American Museum of Natural History, vol 2, New York, 1909; Zitkala-Sa, *Old Indian Legends,* Ginn and Company, Boston, 1901.

For Mother and Bobbie

THE people were hungry. They had walked many days looking for the buffalo herds. Each day they hoped to see the buffalo over the next ridge, but they were not to be found in that part of the country. Even the buzzards and crows circled looking for something to eat, and the wolves called out with hunger at night. The people wandered on until they were too tired and hungry to go any farther, and the dogs could no longer be urged to drag their heavy loads.

The wise men said that they must dance to bring back their relatives, the buffalo. Every man who had dreamed of the buffalo joined in the dance. The buffalo would surely know the people needed them. Young men went out searching in all directions but they did not see any buffalo herds.

There was a boy in the camp who was sad to hear his little brothers and sisters crying with hunger. He saw his mother and father eat nothing so that the children could have what little food there was.

He told his parents: "I am sad to see everyone suffering. The dogs are hungry too. I am going up into the hills to ask the Great Spirit to help us. Do not worry about me; I shall return in the morning."

He left the circle of tipis and walked toward the hills. He climbed higher and higher. The air was cool and smelled fresh with pine trees.

He reached the top of the highest hill as the sun was setting.
He raised his arms and spoke: "Great Spirit, my people need your
help. We follow the buffalo herds because you gave them to us.
But we cannot find them and we can walk no farther. We are
hungry. My little brothers and sisters are crying. Great Spirit, we
need your help."

As he stood there on the hilltop, great clouds closed across the sky. Wind and hail came with sudden force, and behind them Thunderbirds swooped among the clouds. Lightning darted from their flashing eyes and thunder rumbled when they flapped their enormous wings. He felt afraid and wondered if the Great Spirit had answered him.

The clouds parted. Someone came riding toward the boy on the back of a beautiful animal. There was thunder in its nostrils and lightning in its legs; its eyes shone like stars and hair on its neck and tail trailed like clouds.

The boy had never seen any animal so magnificent.

The rider spoke: "I know your people are in need. They will receive this: He is called Sacred Dog because he can do many things your dogs can do, and also more. He will carry you far and will run faster than the buffalo. He comes from the sky. He is as the wind: gentle but sometimes frightening. Look after him always."

The clouds closed and the rider was not there. Suddenly the sky was filled with Sacred Dogs of all colors and the boy could never count their number. Their galloping was like the wind and the drumming of their hoof beats shook the hilltop on which he stood. They circled round and round and he did not know if he was standing or falling.

He did not remember going to sleep, but he awoke as the sun was rising. He knew it was something wonderful he had seen in the sky. He started down the hill back home again to ask the wise men what it meant. They would be able to tell him. The morning and everything around him was beautiful and good.

When the boy had reached the level plain he heard a sound like far-away thunder coming from the hill behind. Looking back he saw Sacred Dogs pouring out of a cave and coming down a ravine toward him. They were of all colors, just as he had seen in the sky, galloping down the slopes, neighing and kicking up their back legs with excitement.

The leading ones stopped when they were a short distance away. They stamped their feet and snorted, but their eyes were gentle too, like those of a deer. The boy knew they were what he had been promised on the hilltop. He turned and continued walking toward the camp and all the Sacred Dogs followed him.

The people were excited and came out from the camp circle when they saw the boy returning with so many strange and beautiful animals. He told them: "These are Sacred Dogs. They are a gift from the Great Spirit. They will help us to follow the buffalo and they will carry the hunters into the running herds. Now there will always be enough to eat. We must look after them well and they will be happy to live with us."

Life was good after that. The people lived as relatives with the Sacred Dogs, together with the buffalo and all other living things, as the Great Spirit wished them to live.

When the people passed the place where they had hunted the buffalo, they would gather up the bleached skulls in a circle and face them toward the sun. "Let us thank the spirits of the buffalo who died so that we could eat."

A Sioux song for the return of the buffalo:

The whole world is coming,
A Nation is coming, a Nation is coming,
The Eagle has brought the message to the tribe,
The Father says so, the Father says so.
Over the whole earth they are coming,
The Buffalo are coming, the Buffalo are coming,
The Crow has brought the message to the tribe,
The Father says so, the Father says so.

Sioux songs of horses:

Friend
my horse
flies like a bird
as it runs.

The four winds are blowing;
some horses
are coming.

Daybreak
appears
when
a horse
neighs.

The Girl Who Loved
Wild Horses

For Janet

THE people were always moving from place to place following the herds of buffalo. They had many horses to carry the tipis and all their belongings. They trained their fastest horses to hunt the buffalo.

There was a girl in the village who loved horses. She would often get up at daybreak when the birds were singing about the rising sun. She led the horses to drink at the river. She spoke softly and they followed.

People noticed that she understood horses in a special way. She knew which grass they liked best and where to find them shelter from the winter blizzards. If a horse was hurt she looked after it.

Every day when she had helped her mother carry water and collect firewood, she would run off to be with the horses. She stayed with them in the meadows, but was careful never to go beyond sight of home.

One hot day when the sun was overhead she felt sleepy. She spread her blanket and lay down. It was nice to hear the horses eating and moving slowly among the flowers. Soon she fell asleep.

A faint rumble of distant thunder did not waken her. Angry clouds began to roll out across the sky with lightning flashing in the darkness beneath. But the fresh breeze and scent of rain made her sleep soundly.

Suddenly there was a flash of lightning, a crash and rumbling which shook the earth. The girl leapt to her feet in fright. Everything was awake. Horses were rearing up on their hind legs and snorting in terror. She grabbed a horse's mane and jumped on his back.

In an instant the herd was galloping away like the wind. She called to the horses to stop, but her voice was lost in the thunder. Nothing could stop them. She hugged her horse's neck with her fingers twisted into his mane. She clung on, afraid of falling under the drumming hooves.

The horses galloped faster and faster, pursued by the thunder and lightning. They swept like a brown flood across hills and through valleys. Fear drove them on and on, leaving their familiar grazing grounds far behind.

At last the storm disappeared over the horizon. The tired horses slowed and then stopped and rested. Stars came out and the moon shone over hills the girl had never seen before. She knew they were lost.

Next morning she was wakened by a loud neighing. A beautiful spotted stallion was prancing to and fro in front of her, stamping his hooves and shaking his mane. He was strong and proud and more handsome than any horse she had ever dreamed of. He told her that he was the leader of all the wild horses who roamed the hills. He welcomed her to live with them. She was glad, and all her horses lifted their heads and neighed joyfully, happy to be free with the wild horses.

The people searched everywhere for the girl and the vanished horses. They were nowhere to be found.

But a year later two hunters rode into the hills where the wild horses lived. When they climbed a hill and looked over the top they saw the wild horses led by the beautiful spotted stallion. Beside him rode the girl leading a colt. They called out to her. She waved back, but the stallion quickly drove her away with all his horses.

The hunters galloped home and told what they had seen. The men mounted their fastest horses and set out at once.

It was a long chase. The stallion defended the girl and the colt. He circled round and round them so that the riders could not get near. They tried to catch him with ropes but he dodged them. He had no fear. His eyes shone like cold stars. He snorted and his hooves struck as fast as lightning.

The riders admired his courage. They might never have caught the girl except her horse stumbled and she fell.

She was glad to see her parents and they thought she would be happy to be home again. But they soon saw she was sad and missed the colt and the wild horses.

Each evening as the sun went down people would hear the stallion neighing sadly from the hilltop above the village, calling for her to come back.

The days passed. Her parents knew the girl was lonely. She became ill and the doctors could do nothing to help her. They asked what would make her well again. "I love to run with the wild horses," she answered. "They are my relatives. If you let me go back to them I shall be happy for evermore."

Her parents loved her and agreed that she should go back to live with the wild horses. They gave her a beautiful dress and the best horse in the village to ride.

The spotted stallion led his wild horses down from the hills. The people gave them fine things to wear: colorful blankets and decorated saddles. They painted designs on their bodies and tied eagle feathers and ribbons in their manes and tails.

In return, the girl gave the colt to her parents. Everyone was joyful.

Once again the girl rode beside the spotted stallion. They were proud and happy together.

But she did not forget her people. Each year she would come back, and she always brought her parents a colt.

And then one year she did not return and was never seen again. But when hunters next saw the wild horses there galloped beside the mighty stallion a beautiful mare with a mane and tail floating like wispy clouds about her. They said the girl had surely become one of the wild horses at last.

Today we are still glad to remember that we have relatives among the Horse People. And it gives us joy to see the wild horses running free. Our thoughts fly with them.

A Navaho's song about his horse:

My horse has a hoof like striped agate;
His fetlock is like a fine eagle-plume;
His legs are like quick lightning.
My horse's body is like an eagle-plumed arrow;
My horse has a tail like a trailing black cloud.
His mane is made of short rainbows.
My horse's ears are made of round corn.
My horse's eyes are made of big stars.
My horse's teeth are made of white shell.
The long rainbow is in his mouth for a bridle,
And with it I guide him.

Black Elk, an Oglala Sioux, had a dream in which he heard a stallion sing a song:

My horses, prancing they are coming.
My horses, neighing they are coming.
Prancing, they are coming.
All over the universe they come.
They will dance; may you behold them.
A horse nation, they will dance,
May you behold them.